MAGIC BED TIME STORIES!

A COLLECTION OF EXCITING AND INSPIRATIONAL STORIES TO FALL ASLEEP QUICKLY

FOR GIRLS AND BOYS

DAVID CONWAY

ISBN – 9798469605072

THIS BOOK BELONGS TO

_ _ _ _ _ _ _ _ _ _ _ _ _ _ _ _ _ _ _

TABLE OF CONTENTS

THE SELFISH ELF

Everyone in Elfland knew that Elvin was the most selfish of all the elves. He never shared any of his toys, especially his favourite spinning top. Whenever anyone asked Elvin if they could play with his toys, he told them that he didn't share.

One day, Elvin was playing outside in front of his house in the middle of Elfland. He lived in a little white house with a pointed brown roof and round windows. Sitting on his front lawn, he was spinning his spinning top over and over, laughing as it whizzed around. He loved to watch the spinning pictures of puppies and ponies.

Suddenly, his spinning top spun off the grass and landed on the gravel path with a clang. Elvin watched in horror as the spinner fell off the bottom and the top landed in pieces.

"No!" Elvin cried out, very upset.

He rushed over to the spinning top to pick it up and started to cry. Holding the pieces of his top, he ran into his house and took them over to his mum.

"Mummy," Elvin cried. "My spinning top is broken. Can you mend it?"

His mother frowned and looked at the top. "Oh, Elvin, I'm sorry. It's too broken to be fixed. Don't worry, you can ask some of the other elves if you can play with their spinning tops."

Her words made him feel better and he decided that it was a good plan. He could still play as long as the other elves shared their spinning tops with him. Right away, he raced out of the house and went to the park where the elves always played. Normally, he never went to the park because he didn't want to share his toys with the other elves. But now, things were different.

When he arrived at the park, he saw all the other elves laughing and having fun with their toys. He noticed Edgar, an elf from his class at school, playing with a bright blue and red spinning top. Elvin ran over to Edgar and waved.

"Hello, Edgar," he said eagerly. "Can I play with you and your spinning top?"

Edgar looked up at him and shook his head. "I'm sorry, Elvin. I'd love to let you play with my spinning top but you never let me play with yours. You always told me that you don't like to share so I won't share with you now."

Elvin remembered all the times he had refused to share his toys with the other elves and he felt bad about it. Now that he knew how horrible it was to be the one who wanted to play, he knew that he should have been nicer.

He wondered if any of the other elves might share with him. He asked lots of the other elves if they would share their toys with him but they all told him the same thing – he had never shared his toys with them, so they wouldn't share their toys with him.

Elvin was just about to leave the park and go home. His head was down in sadness when he heard a voice call his name. Elvin spun around to see Ella; an elf who was a couple of years younger than him. She had long blonde hair and bright blue eyes.

"Hello, Ella," Elvin said.

"You look very sad, Elvin," she told him.

Elvin nodded. "I'm sad because my favourite spinning top broke this morning and nobody will let me play. It's my own fault because I was always so mean and selfish. I would never let anyone play with my toys."

Ella picked up her spinning top from the ground and held it out to him. "You can play with mine if you want," she offered.

Elvin felt very happy and grateful towards Ella. Immediately, he sat down beside her and they started to spin the top. Elvin realised how much fun he was having. He had never thought that it would be more fun to play with someone else than on his own. They spun the top all afternoon until the sun started to set in the sky.

"I should go home for dinner," Ella finally said, standing up and tucking her spinning top under her arm. "Why don't you come back to the park tomorrow and we can play again?"

Nodding, Elvin agreed. He walked all the way home with a giant smile on his face. Ella was so nice to share with him and he felt bad that he could have been having fun all this time with friends instead of being selfish and always playing alone.

When he arrived home, he found his mum and dad in the kitchen. His dad gave him a big hug and handed him a large box.

"Elvin," his dad said. "Your mum told me that your spinning top broke today so I bought you a new one. Now, you can play with it every day."

Elvin was very happy because he knew that he had his own spinning top again so he wouldn't have to share. But then he remembered how much fun he'd had sharing with Ella. Suddenly, Elvin didn't want to keep his toys to himself anymore. He wanted all the elves to have as much fun as he'd had.

The next morning Elvin took his new green and yellow spinning top outside but he didn't sit down on his front lawn to play like he used to do. Instead, he walked to the park with his top. When he got there, the other elves stared at his brand-new spinning top.

Elvin felt a little shy as they all looked at him. "My daddy bought me a new spinning top because my old one broke," he told them all. "But yesterday, I realised that playing with toys is more fun when you have friends. I want you all to play with it."

The elves cheered and rushed over. Elvin held up a hand. "Wait," he said. "I think Ella should have the first spin. Yesterday, she showed me how good it is to share."

Ella jumped up and down excitedly. "Thank you, Elvin," she said with a smile.

Right then, Elvin felt happier than he had ever been before. He had friends now and he didn't want to be selfish anymore. As time went by, Elvin became known throughout Elfland as the kindest and most generous of all the elves and everybody loved him.

THE LAND OF DREAMS

Bertie didn't like to go to bed. Every night he would tell his mummy and daddy that he wasn't tired and he wanted to stay up for as long as possible.

Bertie's mummy and daddy were very tired and upset because they wanted Bertie to be able to enjoy his visits to the Land of Dreams where magical, mystical things happened.

The problem was that Bertie didn't believe in the Land of Dreams. He said that he'd never been so it didn't exist.

"Everyone visits the Land of Dreams when they sleep," Bertie's mum said. "But the pixies and the faeries use magical dust so you don't remember."

"I don't believe you," Bertie said. "I won't sleep."

Bertie refused to sleep even though he was very tired because he had spent all day playing outside with his brother and his sister. As it got darker outside, Bertie became sleepy but he still sat on his bed with his arms folded.

"Bertie," his mum said. "Please go to sleep."

"No!" he insisted with a pout. "I will not sleep."

Bertie stayed awake for a long time but eventually, he could not stay awake any longer. He lay back against his pillows and reluctantly closed his eyes. Within a minute, Bertie was snoring soundly.

* * *

When Bertie opened his eyes, he wasn't in his bed any longer. Instead, he was in a bright clearing in the forest beside a gleaming crystal lake. The sky was bluer and the grass was greener than he had ever seen in his life. Sitting up from where he was lying on the grass, he saw two dragonflies dance around his head and laughed.

"Where am I?" he asked aloud.

Giggles sounded behind him and he spun around to see who was there. Two tiny faeries with golden hair and sparkling wings beamed at him. They fluttered their wings and flew closer.

"You're in the land of dreams," she told him, her voice like tinkling bells. "I'm Annabelle and this is Clarabelle. We knew that you didn't believe in this land so we wanted to show you it's real."

Bertie felt ashamed that he hadn't believed. "Have I been here before?" he asked, realising everything felt familiar.

"You come here every night," Clarabelle said. "But you always come very late because you don't like to go to sleep. So, we don't get a lot of time to have any fun while you're here."

"Yes, we wish you would come earlier," Annabelle said with a nod. "Why don't you like to come here?"

Hanging his head, Bertie fixed his eyes on the ground. "I didn't believe," he told her sadly. "So, I never want to sleep."

"We always wait for you so excitedly," Annabelle replied. "In the future, will you come here earlier?"

"I'll try," Bertie said. "But then, in the morning, I won't remember that I was here."

The two faeries shrugged. "Why don't we dance?" Clarabelle suggested.

"There's no music," Bertie said, glancing around the calm clearing.

As soon as the words left his lips, the most beautiful song he'd ever heard started to play. It wasn't like any kind of music that he'd heard before but the melody made him feel very happy. Without even realising it, he started to dance across the grass. He was having so much fun and he was very glad that he'd finally fallen asleep so he could come here.

Bertie danced with the faeries for hours and hours, laughing and whooping. He gradually noticed that others joined them. Pixies, gnomes, goblins and elves flooded into the clearing and danced around to the music. Lots of animals like bunnies and fawns wandered through the clearing too. Bertie wanted to stay there forever.

Suddenly, Clarabelle clapped her hands. The music began to fade and the other creatures waved goodbye and started to leave. Fluttering her wings, she approached Bertie with a sad smile.

"The night is almost over, Bertie," she said, putting her tiny hand onto his shoulder. "You'll need to go soon and wake up."

"But I don't want to wake up yet," Bertie said. "I won't know I was even here when I wake up. My mum told me that the land of dreams is real and that you'll sprinkle me with dust to make me forget. I didn't believe her but now I know that it's true."

Annabelle raced over to Clarabelle and whispered something to her that Bertie couldn't hear. The two faeries stared at Bertie and sighed.

"We don't normally let little boys and girls wake up without sprinkling our magic dust to make them forget," Annabelle said. "But we're going to make an exception for once. We'll let you remember so that you know why you need to go to sleep at night. It makes your mummy and daddy very sad and worried when you don't want to sleep but you'll want to come here again, won't you?"

"Oh, yes!" Bertie said with a giant smile. "Thank you! I want to remember the land of dreams more than anything."

"Well, it's time to go now," Clarabelle said. "But we'll see you tonight again."

"Bye, Bertie," Annabelle added. "See you soon!"

In the blink of an eye, Bertie found himself back in his bed. Sunlight was streaming through the curtains and he wondered what had just happened. Then, he remembered that he had been in the land of dreams and it was all real. Bertie grinned. From now on, he would be excited to go to bed every single night and visit all his friends in the land of dreams.

He never told anyone about it and he never remembered another visit to the land of dreams but he was sure that he went there every night. Every morning he woke up feeling very happy when he returned from the land of dreams.

BATTLE OF THE PIXIES

For as long as anyone could remember, the Faeries and the Pixies had not liked each other. The Faeries lived in the East and the Pixies lived in the West. But in the middle, there was a big line that divided them.

Nobody knew why they didn't like each other but they always refused to talk to each other if they saw each other at the markets that the two kingdoms shared.

One day, the King of the Pixies and the Queen of the Faeries saw each other at the Royal market that was a big event in the land every year. They glared at each other.

"What are you doing here at this market?" the King of the Pixies asked, narrowing his large brown eyes. "This is *our* market. This is where my pixies buy the most beautiful clothes to wear."

"No," the Queen of the Faeries disagreed, flicking her bright red hair over her shoulder. "This is *our* market. This is where my faeries buy food for our people."

The King shook his head. "Your faeries will never be as good as my pixies."

She disagreed. "Your pixies will never be as good as my faeries."

"You're wrong," he said.

"Well, why don't we have a race and see who is better?" the Queen suggested. "Then it will be settled once and for all."

"Yes, we can race," the Pixie King said.

The Faerie Queen smiled. "Fine. We will have a boat race on the Mystical River and the winner will own the whole land."

Everyone in the land was very excited about the boat race. The pixies were sure that their rowers would win the race and the pixies would be declared the best. The faeries were certain that nobody could beat their rowers in a boat race.

The best rowers had been chosen to take part in the race and they trained every single day as the race approached. They were determined to show that their people were the best.

A large crowd gathered around the shores of the Mystical River as everyone waited for the race to start. The Pixie King and Faerie Queen stood alongside each other. The King was dressed in his finest royal clothes with a deep blue silk coat and his crown on his head. The Queen wore a velvet purple gown, her most beautiful diamond necklace and a golden tiara on her head.

"Are you ready for the pixies to win?" the King asked the Queen.

She glared at him. "Are you ready for the faeries to win?" she retorted.

"We shall see in a few moments," the King replied confidently.

The crowd clapped and cheered as the rowers began to row their boats down the river. The two boats were neck and neck the whole way. They strained and tried their hardest to row as fast as they could.

"My pixies are winning!" the King declared.

"No, they are not," the Queen disagreed. "My faeries are clearly in the lead."

The pixies in the crowd chanted and whooped for their rowers. The faeries clapped and jumped up and down to support their rowers. Everyone held their breath as nobody could tell who was going to win because it looked so close.

As the two boats got closer to the finishing line, there wasn't any space between them. Everyone cried out loudly to try and urge the boat they were supporting over the line. The two boats finished the race at exactly the same time!

"It's a dead heat!" the Pixie King exclaimed. "Our teams crossed the finishing line at the exact same moment!"

The crowd fell silent as they all waited to see what was going to happen now. Even though the pixies and the faeries were two very different groups, they seemed to have been able to row the race in the same amount of time.

The Faerie Queen gasped. "So, we're equally as good as each other?"

"I suppose we are," the King agreed. "I never thought about it before because Pixies and Faeries are so different. But different doesn't mean bad. Now, I know it's possible to be different but equal."

Rising to her feet, the Queen beamed with a smile. "From now on, we will live together in peace and harmony. We can all learn to get along with each other and share our knowledge."

The Faerie Queen's words came true. From that day onwards, the Pixies and the Faeries learned to live alongside each other without fighting. They became friends and shared with each other. Everyone realised that differences could be good because they meant that Pixies and Faeries could learn from each other.

Pixie children and Faerie children went to the same schools and learned together, curious about each other's cultures. As time went by, the Pixies and the Faeries forgot that they used to dislike each other.

Finally, there was no more fighting or war, just joy and happiness.

WHEN TERRY LOST HIS TOADSTOOL

Terry was a goblin with the greenest skin you have ever seen. He had a mane of silvery-white hair and bright jade eyes that sparkled in the sun. He lived in a big red and white toadstool in the woods on the edge of Goblin Town.

Everyone knew how much Terry loved that toadstool and that he never wanted to move to another toadstool. He'd lived there since he was a little goblin and he would often talk about how perfect his toadstool was. He didn't spend much time around the other goblins because he preferred to stay alone in his toadstool.

However, one night a terrible storm hit Goblin Town. All night long the rain pounded, lightning flashed and thunder rumbled in the sky. The mayor of Goblin Town asked all the goblins to be very careful and come out of the woods into the centre of the town so they could be safe.

Terry didn't want to leave the woods or his toadstool but he agreed to stay in the town for the night until the storm was over. In the morning, he was eager to return to his toadstool but when the storm was over and he returned to the woods, he found that his beloved toadstool had been washed away by the storm.

"What am I going to do now?" asked Terry, a tear dripping down his cheek. "I've lived in that Toadstool my whole life and now I have nowhere to live. It was the perfect toadstool and there will never be one as good as it."

The other goblins looked at each other sadly. They all knew that Terry was lost without his toadstool and they didn't know what to do or how to help. For three days and three nights, they all watched as Terry sat in the spot where his toadstool used to be. Everyone could see that he was very sad. So, the goblins talked to each other and decided that they would try and find him a new toadstool.

Every goblin in the town walked around the woods looking for a new toadstool that would make a great home for Terry. They managed to find three different toadstools that looked very promising and they were sure that he would like one of them.

The next morning, the goblins went to the spot where Terry was sitting and smiled at him to cheer him up. Eloise was a young goblin with long blonde hair and jade coloured skin. She stepped forward to Terry very excitedly.

"We have found some new toadstools for you to look at, Terry," Eloise said to him with a bright smile. "Why don't you come with us and see if you like them?"

Terry looked very unsure. "But I liked my old toadstool," he replied. "I won't ever see another toadstool that is as good as my old one."

Eloise sat down beside him on the log. "I know," she said sympathetically. "We're very sad that you lost your toadstool but why don't you come with us and see the new ones?"

Reluctantly, Terry agreed to go and look at the new toadstools. The goblins led him through the woods to look at the first toadstool. It was a little toadstool with a pale red cap and cream spots.

"It's too small," Terry said with a frown. "I don't like it."

Eloise sighed. "It's okay, Terry. We have another toadstool to look at."

They walked further into the woods towards the second toadstool. It was a huge deep red toadstool with giant white spots.

"No, this one is not right either," Terry whined, staring at the giant toadstool. "It's far too big."

Eloise was starting to lose hope that he would like any of their toadstools. "Are you sure?" she asked. "You would have lots of space here."

Terry looked sad. "I don't want to live here," he said firmly. "It's nothing like my old toadstool. My old toadstool was perfect."

"Alright, Terry," Eloise replied. "Well, we still have one more toadstool to look at."

The goblins walked a little further and Eloise pointed to a beautiful velvety crimson coloured toadstool with furry white spots across the top. Terry stared at it in awe. It was the loveliest looking toadstool he had ever seen in his whole life.

"Do you like it?" Eloise asked nervously.

Terry walked around the toadstool, looking at its beautiful red top and bright white spots. "Yes," he agreed. "I think this might be the one."

Eloise cheered joyfully. "I'm so glad," she said. "We worked so hard to find the perfect toadstool for you, Terry."

The goblins spent the rest of the day bringing the furniture to the toadstool so that Terry could be comfortable there. He was very surprised at how much everyone wanted to help him. He had never spent much time with the other goblins because he had always wanted to be alone in his old toadstool but he felt so happy that they all wanted to help him when he needed it. He felt very special.

It warmed Terry's heart to know that all the people in his village had worked together to help find the perfect new toadstool for him. All his life, he'd lived alone in the toadstool but now he knew that working together with others was a good thing that could bring him amazing benefits.

Terry thanked all the other goblins before they went back to their own homes and told them that he was very grateful for all their help.

He lay down on his new bed and glanced around his brand-new toadstool. "I think it's even better than my old one," he said to himself with a smile, before falling into a peaceful sleep.

LILY'S LUCKY LEPRECHAUN

Lily was a young girl of seven years old. She had fiery red hair and bright green eyes. She loved to play with her friends outside and run around in the sun. The only problem was that Lily's family had just moved to a new town and she had left all her friends behind in her old town.

As she sat outside in the field that ran behind her house, Lily felt very sad. None of the children in her new town seemed to want to be her friend and nobody talked to her at school. She missed her old friends and she wished that she could go back and be with them again.

Lily's mummy and daddy told her that she needed to be more confident and she would find some friends but Lily was very shy when she was around people she didn't know.

One Saturday afternoon, Lily's mummy asked her to take the rubbish outside. Lily was going to do it but she was playing with her puppy, Alfie and she forgot. A little later that afternoon, she remembered what her mum had asked but when she went to the door, it was raining very hard outside. Lily was worried because she didn't want to get wet but she didn't want her mum to be angry at her for forgetting to do her chores.

Lily decided that she would wait a little while until it stopped raining and then she would finish her chores then. After an hour the rain cleared and the sun came out brightly in the sky. Lily grabbed the bag of rubbish and headed out into the garden. As she looked up, she saw the most beautiful sight that she had ever seen. There was a stunning rainbow overhead with colours like red, orange, yellow, green, blue, indigo and violet.

Suddenly, Lily heard a rumble coming from the rainbow and saw a small man tumble down it onto the ground just like he was on a slide at the park. Lily gasped loudly as she watched him stand up and brush the dust off his clothes, grumbling to himself all the while.

She stared at the small man, looking at his round, kindly face, velveteen emerald trousers and jacket. On his head, he wore a hat that was as green as the grass and had a large brown buckle on the top. He stroked his short beard as he stared back at her just as surprised to see her as she was to see him.

"Well, now," he said in an Irish accent. "I didn't expect a little girl to be at the end of my rainbow."

Lily took a step backwards. "Who are you?" she asked. "What are you doing in my garden."

He grinned at her, placing a large green pot down next to him. The pot was brimming with chunks of gold. "I'm Leo the leprechaun," he told her. "I think I took a wrong turn because this wasn't where I'm supposed to be."

"Oh, I'm Lily," she said with a sigh. "I'm sorry you're lost."

Leo's face turned from happy to sad as he looked at her thoughtfully. "I'm always doing things wrong. I try very hard to bring luck to people but I'm not good at it."

"I'm sure you are," she reassured him. "Maybe you just don't realise it."

Leo shrugged. "So, what are you doing out in your garden alone on a Saturday?" he asked her. "Why are you not with your friends?"

"I don't have any friends," Lily replied. "I'm too shy to talk to people I don't know."

Laughing, Leo shook his head. "But you're talking to me," he reminded her. "So, you must be able to talk to the other kids at your school. Have you tried?"

"Not really," she admitted. "I'm scared to talk to anyone in case they don't like me."

Leo took off his hat and tucked it under his arm. "Lily, it can be hard to do things when you're afraid. Sometimes, you just have to try." He reached into the green pot and fished out a piece of gold, handing it to her. "This will give you some luck. I don't know if it will work because I'm not very good at my job but please try it and show an old leprechaun that he can bring a little luck."

Lily nodded and took the gold with a grateful smile. "Thank you, Leo."

"Well, I should be going," Leo said, picking up his pot of gold. "Just remember to keep that gold with you all the time and you'll have all the luck you need."

Before Lily could reply, Leo jumped onto the rainbow and whooshed out of sight. Lily stared down at the piece of gold in her hand and hoped it would bring her some luck.

When Lily went back to school on Monday, she was very nervous but she had her piece of gold with her and she felt lucky. As she sat down at her desk, she noticed a blonde girl sitting next to her. She didn't recognise the girl.

"Hi," Lily said quietly, turning to the girl. "I'm Lily. Are you new in school?"

The girl nodded shyly. "Yes," she whispered. "I'm Jessica and this is my first day. I don't know anyone here at this school."

Lily couldn't believe her luck that she'd met someone else who was new in school. Feeling more confident with her piece of gold, she smiled at Jessica. "Would you like to be friends?" Lily asked.

Jessica broke out into a beaming smile. "I'd love to! Let's each lunch together."

Lily was very happy. She knew that Leo had really brought her luck but she also knew that finding the confidence to talk to Jessica had come from within. His little spark of magic had let her get over her shyness and finally find a friend.

A few weeks later, Leo decided to visit Lily at her school and check to see how she was doing on her quest to find friends. He hopped onto his rainbow and slid down to the end that led to her schoolyard. Leo hid behind the tree and watched Lily talking with some other girls. He was very happy that she had made friends.

The girls were laughing together very loudly and it made his heart feel warm. Right then, he realised something very important. He *could* bring good luck. By spending time with Lily and helping her find out that she had confidence, even though she didn't think so, he'd brought her lots of luck and helped her find friends.

Waving to Lily, Leo hopped onto the end of the rainbow and whooshed over to the other side. There were lots of other children that needed his help and he would be there for all of them to help them just like he helped Lily.

MARLA THE MERMAID

Marla the mermaid loved living in the oceans and exploring far and wide. Her parents sometimes worried about her because they knew that humans often liked to catch mermaids and take them out of the seas.

"Please do not go too far away from home," her mother warned her. "Most importantly, do not go to the South Sea. There are many humans there and they will catch you."

Marla thought that her mother was very silly to worry. She didn't think that humans would ever catch her because she could swim too fast and she was sure that she was much quicker than any of the humans.

She'd only ever met a human once. It was many years ago when she was only a small mermaid. A little human boy had swum too far out to sea and he was very scared. Marla had helped to rescue him and had taken him back to shore. He had been very nice so she thought that humans must all be very nice too.

So, Marla ignored her mother's words and decided that she wanted to see the South Sea for herself. The South Sea was on the far side of the ocean, a very long way away from where she lived. Marla didn't care that it would be a long journey because it was very exciting.

The morning that she decided she wanted to set off for the South Sea, she brushed her long blonde wavy hair and put on her best purple shell top. Flicking her tail, she went on her way toward the South Sea.

It took Marla several hours to get to where she was going and she was very tired when she finally arrived. She had expected the South Sea to be a very exciting place but, to her disappointment, it was very dull instead. There were some crabs, fish, and a few basking sharks but she couldn't see much else. It was just like her home and not the magical place that she had imagined it would be.

Feeling annoyed that she'd wasted her time, Marla decided to turn around and go home. Suddenly, just as she was about to leave, she felt a net close around her tail. Marla tried to get out of the net but she couldn't because it was too tight.

As Marla looked up, she saw the bottom of a boat and realised that she'd been trapped in a human net. Marla began to panic. No matter how hard she struggled, she couldn't get out of the net. She felt even worse as she felt the net raising her from the water. She wished that she'd listened to her mother and not come to the South Sea.

Before Marla knew what was happening, the net pulled her out of the water and she sprawled onto the hard wooden planks of a fishing boat. Marla was dazed. She looked around and saw a man standing over her in shock.

"It's you," the man whispered.

Marla shrank back, feeling scared. "I want to go back to the water," she mumbled. "Please let me go."

The man didn't reply but he crouched down and Marla had her first chance to look at him. Strangely, he seemed familiar though she didn't know any humans. The only one she'd ever met had been the little boy that she'd rescued all those years ago. Then she realised that this was the same human. He was older now, a man, but it was the same person. She couldn't forget his jet-black curls or his hazel eyes.

"You're real," the man said. "I thought I imagined you but you *do* exist. I don't know if you remember me but you saved me from the ocean when I was just a small boy."

Marla nodded. "I remember. But I don't understand why you would want to take me out of the ocean."

"I thought you were a fish," the man explained, laughing with embarrassment. "I'm a fisherman and you got caught in my net. What are you doing here?"

"I wanted to explore the South Sea. My mother told me not to because she said that humans capture mermaids here."

"Your mother is very wise," the man replied. "You should have listened to her. All those years ago, my mother warned me not to swim too far out to sea and I didn't listen either and I ended up in a lot of trouble. It was only you that kept me safe."

Marla chuckled softly. "I guess our parents are wiser than we are."

The man agreed with a nod. "I'll untangle you from the net," he offered, cutting the ropes. "Go back home and be more careful in the future. Many fishermen wouldn't return you to the sea."

"I suppose I'm lucky," she said.

"Just like I was lucky when you saved me," he replied, smiling. "I'm glad I finally got the chance to return the favour."

Marla waved the man goodbye as she dived back into the warm waters of the ocean. She was very relieved to be free again and she knew that she'd been silly when she refused to listen to her mother's warnings. She also felt happy that the little boy she'd rescued many years ago had grown up to be a kind man and that warmed her heart.

Swimming all the way home without stopping, Marla realised that it was fun to have an adventure but she needed to be sensible in the future. She would listen to her mother and do kind deeds when people needed them. Kindness made the world go around.

THE SCARED LITTLE BEAR CUB

It was a very warm day in the woods. The big orange sun shined brightly in the clear sky. Brandon the bear cub sat by the large blue lake watching all his siblings having fun. The other bears were swimming in the lake and laughing very loudly and happily. But Brandon didn't feel happy. He felt sad.

Brandon wanted to swim in the lake like his brothers and sisters but he was too scared. He'd tried to swim many times but he had never been able to make it into the water because of his fear. It was very hot sitting by the side of the lake but he didn't want to go into the rippling water, even though it looked very nice.

"Brandon!" called his oldest sister, Bella as she padded out of the water. "Why don't you come into the lake? It's so nice and cool in there and it's too hot out here in the sun."

Brandon shook his head. "You know that I don't like the water, Bella," he said sadly. "I will stay here and watch you all play in the lake."

Bella walked closer to him and brushed a paw over his shoulder. "Brandon, you will have to overcome your fear of the water someday," she told him. "You cannot be scared forever. Mum and Dad are very upset that you don't want to swim. How will you ever fish in the river for food if you cannot go into the water?"

He didn't know what to say to his sister. He felt very ashamed that he could not swim. As far as he knew, no other bears were scared of swimming, like he was.

At that moment, his father came out of the cave where they all lived. The older bear noticed Brandon and Bella sitting by the edge of the lake and he walked over to them. He smiled at his cubs and sat down beside them.

"Are you not going to swim?" he asked Brandon.

"I do not want to go into the water, Dad," Brandon said. "It scares me."

His dad sighed. "Why don't you try, Son? I'll go in with you and everything will be fine. There is nothing to be scared of. You've seen all of us swimming in the lake and there is no reason for you to have so much fear."

"I'm sorry, Dad," Brandon said. "I don't think that I will ever be able to go into the water."

Brandon stood up and felt even sadder than before as he walked away toward the cave. He didn't like to feel like a wimp. His brothers and sisters seemed to have no problems at all with the water and they were never scared. But he *was*. Whenever he watched them in the water, he felt very jealous that he could not bring himself to climb into the water.

When he was a younger cub, Brandon had really tried to get into the water but he got scared whenever he was close to it. He didn't even know why he was scared. He remembered how hard his mum had tried to get him to go into the water. She was very disappointed that her youngest bear was such a scaredy-cub.

Going into his cave, he was glad to be out of the heat of the sun. He sat down in the corner alone and peered out at his brothers and sisters having fun outside. Finally, he fell asleep and dreamed that he would someday, somehow be able to go into the lake without being afraid.

* * *

The next day, Brandon's mum and dad woke him up very early. They seemed really excited and Brandon wondered what was going on. He looked around the cave and he noticed that his mum was packing some things into a suitcase.

"What's going on?" Brandon asked, still sleepy.

His mother came over to him and gave him a big smile. "We're going down to the river for a few days," she told him. "We want to go and find some food."

When he heard that they were going to the river, Brandon felt very afraid. He knew that they would want him to go into the water and he would not be able to do that.

Brandon gulped. "I don't want to come."

His mother looked upset and frowned. "You have to come, Brandon," she said. "You can't stay in the cave and not come to get food."

"Can you not bring some food back for me?" he asked, pleading with her.

His father padded over and stood next to his mother. "Do you really not want to come?" he asked Brandon.

Brandon shook his head. "I don't like the river, Dad. I won't be able to go into the water and it will make me sad."

"Someday, you will have to go into the water," his father reminded him. "When you grow up, you will need to go into the river to find food." He paused, thinking. "But this time, you can stay here, if you really want. Your sister, Bella, will stay with you though. You are too little to stay on your own."

Brandon felt very relieved. But, as he watched his family leave on their trip, he also felt very sad and lonely. Bella was outside, swimming in the lake again and he had nobody to talk to.

Later in the afternoon, Bella came into the cave and yawned. "I'm so tired," she said, lying down on the ground at the far side of the cave. "Playing in the lake all day has made me feel very sleepy. It was so much fun but I think I need a nap now."

Before Brandon could reply, he noticed that his sister was already fast asleep and snoring loudly. Brandon sighed. He decided that he would go out for a walk to make himself feel better. He went outside and noticed that the air was still very warm. The woods smelled of sweet summer flowers and he tried to think about how nice it was out there but he couldn't stop thinking that he wished he wasn't a scaredy-cub.

As he walked by the lake, he noticed a little human boy and girl playing by the edge of the water. Smiling, he realised that he liked hearing their sounds of laughter as they splashed around and had fun. For a long time, he watched them from behind a tree. He thought that they might be scared if they saw him.

Suddenly, he saw the little boy slip and fall into the water. Brandon felt very upset and worried.

"Help!" the little boy cried.

On the bank of the lake, the girl was crying but she was too little to help her brother. Brandon didn't know what to do. He thought about going to get Bella but he knew that she was fast asleep inside the cave. There was nobody else around and Brandon knew that he was the only one that could help.

Without thinking about his fear, Brandon raced forward toward the water and dived in. The water felt very cool against his skin. He swam over to the little boy and nudged him onto his back. Paddling over to the bank, he set him onto the green grass.

"You saved my brother!" the little girl said happily, giving Brandon a big hug. He saw how grateful she was and it made Brandon's heart swell with happiness.

Just at that moment, he saw the children's parents rushing over through the woods. Brandon knew they must have heard the little boy cry out for help. He didn't want them to be scared of him so he rushed away and hid. He saw the boy's mummy and daddy give him a big hug and he knew that the little boy was fine. Brandon felt very relieved.

For a little while, he watched the family as they packed up their stuff and got into a car. Once they had left the woods, Brandon was alone. Then he realised something amazing.

He had been able to swim in the lake.

When Brandon had seen the little boy in danger, he had overcome all of his fears. He'd found the courage to dive in and save the child. Swimming was the one thing that he'd never thought he would be able to do but now he knew that he wasn't a wimp. He was a brave, strong bear, not a scaredy-cub.

Brandon felt very proud of himself. He had faced his fears and helped someone. Now, he knew that he could do anything he set his mind to do without feeling scared. Brandon wasn't sad anymore. He was very happy.

From that day on, Brandon often swam in the lake with his siblings. His mum and dad wondered what had changed but they were very glad that he was able to go into the water. Brandon was very glad too. He would never be a scaredy-cub again.

JOHNNY'S FLYING HORSE

Johnny loved to ride horses but he wasn't very good at it. He often competed against the other children in competitions but he never won. Johnny became very angry that he didn't win and he wanted to find a way to be the best horse rider in the whole town.

His dad told him that he needed to practise more but Johnny was a very lazy boy and he didn't care to spend time practising. He just wanted to win!

One day, he'd just come last in a jumping competition and he was really upset. He walked around the fields feeling very down.

"It's not fair!" he grumbled. "Why should I have to practise horse jumping to be good at it? I wish there was an easy way to be good!"

At that moment, Johnny heard a rumble in the sky and a huge beast swooped down from overhead. As he got his bearings, Johnny stared at the creature and he realised that it was a majestic white horse with giant wings. The horse tucked its wings back into its side and nodded its head at Johnny.

"You're a horse," Johnny whispered. "And you can fly!"

"My name is Vol," the horse told him. "And yes, I can fly."

"You can talk too?" Johnny asked in awe.

Vol nodded again. "I was flying overhead and I heard you talking to yourself. I know that you want to be good at horse jumping and I thought that I might be able to help. I can run very fast and jump very high."

Johnny was very excited. This would be an easy way for him to win a horse jumping competition without having to practise at all. He jumped at Vol's offer. "I have a competition next week. Will you help me?"

"Of course, I will. You'll see exactly what I can do," Vol said with a slight smile.

The next week passed by very quickly and Johnny didn't even bother to visit the stables at all. He thought that he didn't need to because he'd found an easy way to win. When the day of the competition rolled around, Vol met Johnny in front of the fields.

"I'm glad you're here," Johnny said. "Today is the day that I'm finally going to win."

Vol didn't say anything but he crouched down so that Johnny could climb onto his back. "Are you ready?" Vol asked.

"Absolutely," Johnny replied.

The horse and his rider strode out onto the riding course. There were lots of people in the crowd including Johnny's mum, dad and his two older sisters. He knew that nobody thought he would win but today he was going to prove them all wrong.

Johnny heard the timer start and Vol took off very fast. Johnny had to cling tightly onto his back so that he didn't fall off as Vol raced around the course, jumping every fence with ease. When he finished, Johnny was panting and a little scared. However, he was very happy because he knew that he had won.

As the crowd cheered, Vol spread his gigantic wings and everyone fell silent. Johnny realised what had happened and saw every pair of eyes was on him.

"He has a flying horse!" someone called from the crowd. "He's a cheat!"

"Cheat! Cheat! Cheat!" the crowd chanted.

Johnny was mortified and he jumped off Vol's back and sped into the stables where he could be alone. He didn't understand why Vol would show him up like that. He'd been so happy that he'd won and now he looked foolish in front of the whole town. Everyone would know he'd tried to cheat to win.

Vol padded into the stables and Johnny stared at him, very unhappy. "Why did you show me up like that?" Johnny asked.

Sighing, Vol shuffled over to Johnny. "I wanted to show you that you cannot get anywhere in life by cheating, Johnny. I've been watching you for a while and I know you're a talented horse jumper but you wanted to be lazy and take the easy way out. So, I showed you there is *never* an easy way out. Cheaters never prosper."

"But now I look like a fool in front of the whole town," Johnny whined.

Vol shook his head. "Luckily for you, I have a very good friend who's a pixie and she's sprinkled forgetfulness dust over everyone so they will not remember what happened. But *you* will remember and I hope you will learn from it for the future."

Johnny nodded very quickly, feeling relieved. "Oh, yes! I promise you that I will never do anything so silly again. In the future, I'll work hard and not be lazy."

Vol seemed satisfied by what Johnny said but he raised his brows. "Remember that I'll be watching you, Johnny," he said before he spread his wings and soared off into the sky.

Johnny walked out of the stables and he knew that he'd had a lucky escape. He could easily have been the laughing stock of the town and nobody would ever have trusted him again if they thought he was a cheat. But he also knew that he had to keep his promise to Vol and never cheat again. He felt guilty that he had tried to cheat in the first place and he knew it was the wrong thing to do.

From that day on, Johnny worked very hard to become a good horse jumper. He practised every evening after school and all weekend. As time went by, he got better and better and started to finish higher in the rankings when he took part in contests.

After almost a year, Johnny finally won his first competition. He felt very proud of himself because he knew that all of his hard work had paid off. His family was very proud too and everyone congratulated him.

As he stared down at the small gold medal around his neck, he heard a fluttering of wings overhead. Looking up, Johnny saw Vol in the sky and he smiled. If it were not for the flying horse, he would never have learned the value of hard work and he was truly grateful. He knew that he would never be lazy and never try to cheat again.

A BROKEN ENGINE

Max was a steam engine who lived in Mr Carter's trainyard. He remembered when he had been the talk of the town. There had been a time when he was young and everyone wanted him to pull their carriages.

Back then, he had travelled the length and breadth of the country, pulling carriages all day long. Everyone had admired his bright red body and they often told him how good he looked. He had always been proud of how fast he could travel.

Then, times had changed. New engines had come along and he had been replaced by the young electric engines. The electric engines ran on the power lines that made them very quick. Nobody wanted to use a slow old steam engine anymore and now he sat in the trainyard all day long, ignored and forgotten. Even his red coat, which he had always been very proud of, was peeling and sad-looking.

Max really missed the old days when he had been useful and beautiful. When he was young, he had never sat still for more than a few minutes. Every day, he had travelled to so many amazing places and seen all the beautiful parts of the country. He didn't like sitting around all day. He wished that he could just have one or two journeys to make but when he asked Mr Carter, he said no.

"I'm sorry, Max," Mr Carter said firmly. "We just don't need to use a steam engine now. The electric engines are so much faster than you."

"But I can still pull carriages," Max said sadly. "I could be really useful if you would let me try."

Evan, one of the younger electric engines heard the conversation and laughed at Max. "Yeah!" he said meanly. "Why would Mr Carter want to use you? You're old and useless and you can't travel quickly as *we* can."

Another of the electric engines, Ethan, joined Evan in his laughter. "You shouldn't even be in the trainyard anymore," he chuckled. "Nobody will use you to pull their carriages ever again."

That night, Max cried himself to sleep in his shed. He felt very lonely and sad, knowing that nobody wanted to be friends with an old, worn-out engine like him. He really wished things were different but he could not see any way that things would change.

* * *

The next morning, Mr Carter came rushing into the train yard. He was humming with excitement and clapped his hands together to get the attention of all the engines. The engines fell silent and stared at him.

"Well, I have just heard the best news," Mr Carter told them with a big smile on his face. "I just got a call from the Royal Palace. There is going to be a very big party next week and they want to use our engines to take all the food and supplies to the palace."

A hum of excitement rippled through the engines. "I bet that I'll be chosen to pull the carriages," Ethan boasted.

"Me too!" Evan giggled.

Mr Carter nodded. "Of course," he said. "You are our best engines, Ethan and Evan. I trust you to transport this very important cargo. The party at the palace is going to be really big so we must get the food there on time."

"That will be easy for me," Evan said, sounding very relaxed. "I won't even need to break a sweat."

"I'll be even faster," Ethan added.

Max watched the excitement of the other engines and he felt so left out. He knew that, no matter what, he wouldn't be a part of it. Why would they want to use an old steam engine to take such important things to the palace? He felt a tear run down his cheek and went to hide inside his shed.

* * *

The big day of the royal party approached very fast. As it got closer, all the trains were so excited but Max felt sadder and sadder. It was hard to hear them talking about how wonderful it would be when he knew that he wasn't going to be a part of it.

53

The night before the party, Max stayed in his shed, staring out at the darkness. Suddenly, he saw a flash of light and heard a rumble of thunder. The rain started to pour down outside. It was a terrible storm and Max was a little scared. It had been hot weather all day and he knew that storms often happened when it had been too hot outside. He hoped that the storm would not cause too much damage though. He didn't want a tree to come down on the train lines.

Max didn't sleep much that night. Instead, he just watched the storm and thought about the days when he had been young and everyone admired and liked him. It seemed like such a long time ago now. He wondered if the young engines knew that they would grow older someday too.

Finally, as morning came, the storm cleared. All the engines were very relieved as they did not want to get wet and carry the food to the palace in such a bad storm. But just then, Mr Carter rushed into the train yard in a panic.

"Oh, engines, I had some bad news and I don't know what I'm going to do," he cried, rushing this way and that. "Last night's storm caused a power cut across the whole country and none of the power lines are working. That means that none of you will be able to run on the train lines."

Worried whispers rushed through the electric engines. Max glanced around and they all looked very upset.

"What are we going to do?" Evan cried. "I was looking forward to taking the food to the Royal Palace."

Mr Carter shook his head. "I don't know," he said. "If we do not get the food to the palace, the party will be ruined and my trains will be a laughing stock."

Max watched them from inside his shed and he had a sudden idea. Rolling forward, he coughed and cleared his throat. "I have a suggestion," he said shyly.

Mr Carter and the trains turned around to face him. "What is your idea?" the trainyard owner asked.

Max took a breath. "Unlike the electric engines, I do not need a power line to run on. I can run on coal and wood. So, even with the power lines down, I could pull the carriages to the Royal Palace."

The other engines roared with laughter at his suggestion. He could see that Evan and Ethan thought he was silly to say such a thing.

"You haven't been used in so long that you probably won't even work anymore," Evan said.

"I still want to try," Max insisted, ignoring their mean laughter.

Mr Carter looked unsure but he nodded. "Okay, Max," he agreed. "I guess we don't have any other choice. We'll let you try and see what you can do."

Max was very excited. As the engine driver climbed on board and stoked him up with fuel, he felt like he had been brought back to life. Chugging forward toward the line, he creaked and groaned but he hadn't forgotten how to move along the tracks. As Mr Carter hooked the carriages full of food to him, Max was very determined that he would not fail. He could do this.

When the engine driver sounded Max's whistle, Max felt happier than he had been in years. He set off slowly along the train tracks. At first, he was a little wobbly but it didn't take long before he got back into the swing of things. He chugged down the tracks and laughed as he remembered just how good it felt to travel.

"We need to go a little faster!" the engine driver called. "We don't have much time. Can you manage it?"

"I can do it!" Max agreed.

Speeding up, they whooshed past the scenery and Max loved the feeling of the breeze in his face. This was the very best day of his life.

Finally, they arrived at the train station close to the Royal Palace. Lots of people were waiting on the platform to collect the food from the carriages. The engine driver hopped down and stared at Max in admiration, just like people used to do when he was young.

"You did a good job," the driver said. "I'm proud of you. I'm sure that Mr Carter will give you a bright new coat of paint now too."

Max grinned and hoped that people would like him now that he had shown them just what he could do.

* * *

When Max returned to the trainyard, he didn't expect the welcome that he got. Everyone cheered proudly and even Evan and Ethan seemed in awe of him.

"You're a hero across the land," Mr Carter told him. "You saved the royal party. It would have been ruined if you hadn't taken that food there."

Evan smiled at Max. "I always thought that being old meant that you couldn't do things anymore," he admitted. "But now I know that I was wrong. I'm sorry."

"I'm sorry too," Ethan said. "We were wrong to ignore your skills and we should have given you more respect."

Max accepted their apologies and he felt very proud of himself. He knew that he could still do all the things that he used to do. Just because he was older, that didn't mean he should be ignored.

From that day on, Mr Carter let Max go out on special trips every day. Max had the new job of pulling carriages full of happy schoolchildren around the country, taking them on sightseeing tours. It made Max feel joyful. The younger engines gave him lots of respect and even asked for his advice sometimes. Max even got his bright new red coat of paint and that made him feel very glad because he looked so shiny and new again.

Max had finally found a purpose and he didn't have to sit idly in the trainyard anymore. This was what he was made for and he had never been happier.

ANNIE AND THE DUCKLINGS

Annie loved to play outside in her garden with her older sister, Sarah. She loved the way the warm sun felt on her skin. One morning, she woke up very early and went out into the garden on her own. For a little while, she ran around but she thought that it was boring to play on her own.

Suddenly, she saw something moving at the end of the garden and she walked over to see what it was. As she got closer, she noticed four little ducklings huddled together under the shade of a bush.

"Hello, little duckies," she said, approaching them carefully because she didn't want to scare them.

The ducklings looked up at her very pitifully. They looked very thin and not well at all. They seemed so hungry and lost that Annie knew she had to help them.

"Wait here, please," she told the ducklings before running into the house.

When she got inside, her mum, dad and sister were sitting in the kitchen, just about to eat breakfast. Her mum was making some pancakes at the stove and her sister was drinking a large glass of orange juice. On the other side of the table, her dad was reading the newspaper. He put the newspaper down to look at her.

"Good morning, Annie," he said with a smile.

"Morning, Daddy," she replied.

"What were you doing in the garden so early?" her mum asked, ladling some pancake batter into a pan.

Annie was still breathless from running all the way up the garden. "I woke up early," she told her mum. "I went outside to play in the garden and I just found some ducklings on their own. They don't seem well. They're very thin and they look like they're lost."

"Oh dear," said her father, shaking his head. "That's very sad."

"I know!" Annie agreed. "Can I keep them and make them better?"

Annie's mum looked unsure. "I don't know if that's a good idea," she said, placing some delicious pancakes down on the table. Annie's tummy rumbled because they smelled so good but she could only think about helping the ducklings.

Sarah sat upright in her chair. "Oh, mummy, please can we keep them?" she piped up. "I'd love to have some ducklings as pets!"

Their father glanced at their mum. "Having a pet is a lot of responsibility, girls," he said. "Besides, ducks are wild animals. They like to roam free."

"But these ducklings have lost their mummy," Annie protested. "If we don't help them something bad could happen to them. I would be very sad if I lost my mummy and nobody helped me."

Annie's mum nodded. "Okay," she said. "You can keep them for now until they are all better. But they won't be able to stay here forever, Annie. Someday they will grow up into ducks and they will have to leave."

Annie and Sarah both nodded. They knew that the ducklings couldn't stay forever but the girls were glad that they could look after them for now. Annie led her family outside and her mum and dad carefully picked up the ducklings and put them into the shed which was nice and warm and had a window so they could get lots of air and light. Their mum brought them some food and water so they wouldn't be hungry or thirsty anymore.

Over the next few weeks, Annie and Sarah nursed the ducklings back to health. Their mum and dad were very proud that they took such good care of the ducks. Annie named them all: Fred, Hannah, Michael and Leah.

Fred was the leader of the ducklings and the bravest. Annie noticed that he seemed to be the one in charge of his duckling siblings and they followed his lead. Hannah was a lot shier but she loved to cuddle with Annie and Sarah. Michael was always the greediest duckling and would come running over to the girls as soon as they brought food. Leah was the most relaxed and she liked to play games and hide the food from Michael as a joke.

Annie knew that the ducklings would grow up someday and go away but she wished that she could keep them with her forever. She was very glad they seemed strong and happy now though. They had really changed and grown from the lost little ducklings they had been when she first found them in her garden.

One morning, she had just finished feeding the ducklings and went out of the shed when she saw a large duck at the end of the garden. She realised that it was Mummy Duck. She saw the sad look on Mummy Duck's face and she knew right away that she had come to take her ducklings.

Annie started to panic. She knew that Mummy Duck was very sad without her ducklings but Annie didn't want to let them go. Quickly, she ran into the shed and scooped the ducklings into her arms. She carried them into the house and took them upstairs to her bedroom.

Annie kept the ducklings in her room for a week. She felt very guilty because she saw Mummy Duck waiting in the garden every time she looked out of the window. Sarah asked her what had happened to the ducklings and Annie pretended that she didn't know.

A few days later, Annie's mum came into her bedroom and saw the ducklings. "Annie!" she said angrily. "What are the ducklings doing in here? I thought you didn't know where they were. You lied to us and that's very wrong."

Annie was very ashamed that she'd lied and she knew that she had done the wrong thing. "I'm sorry, Mummy," she said, starting to cry. "I saw their mummy in the garden and I knew that she had come to take them away. The ducklings are my friends and I didn't want to lose them."

Annie's mum sighed. She was still angry at Annie for lying but she felt sorry that Annie was going to have to say goodbye to the ducklings.

"It's always wrong to lie, Annie," her mother explained. "You should never lie, even if you think you are doing it for the right reasons. But you have to let the ducklings go back to their mummy. Mummy Duck loves her ducklings, just like I love you and your sister. She's very sad without them."

Annie sighed. "I'll miss them," she said, pouting.

"I know," her mum replied. "But their mummy misses them even more. It took great strength and courage to rescue the ducklings and nurse them back to health but it will take even greater strength to let them go. Sometimes doing the right thing is very difficult but it is worth it in the end."

At that moment, Annie understood that she had to give the ducklings back to their mummy. It would be hard to say goodbye but she could be strong. She knew then that she was never supposed to keep the ducklings forever. Her job was to keep them safe for their mother.

Annie carried the ducklings down the stairs and took them out into the garden. As soon as they saw their mother, they ran to her, chirping loudly and brushing against her. Annie waved to the ducks as they all toddled off. Mummy Duck lingered for a moment and Annie was sure that she gave her a grateful smile. Annie realised that her mum was right. Doing the right thing was hard but it was worth it. She knew that she had done an amazing thing and she would never forget the ducklings.

THE LITTLEST GIANT

George the giant hated being small. All the other giants were very big and they could do anything that they wanted but he was the littlest giant in the whole land. When the other giants were able to reach up almost to the sky, George didn't like it because he wasn't like them.

Sometimes, a human would wander into their lands and that made George feel better because humans were small like he was. There were times when he wished that he lived in the human world so he wouldn't feel so small.

"Being a little giant is not a bad thing," his older brother Gerry told him.

"You don't understand," George replied. "You're very tall so you can never know what it's like to be a little giant. I don't fit in with all the other giants here."

One day the Giant King called all the giants to a meeting in the town square. George didn't want to go because he always felt so small when he was around lots of other giants. He didn't think that he could ever be good enough when he wasn't tall like all the others.

"You can't stay here feeling sorry for yourself," Gerry said. "Why don't you come into the town with me so we can hear what the king has to say. It must be important because the king rarely calls all the giants together like this."

George reluctantly tagged along beside his brother as they walked into the town. When they arrived, a large crowd had already gathered in the huge central square. They waited for the king and George looked around at all the other giants. They towered over him and George felt very small compared to them.

Suddenly, the crowd cheered as the king walked out onto the stage in front of the Royal Palace. George jumped up and down, trying to catch a glimpse of the king. Sadly, he could not see anything because all the giants in front of him were too tall for him to see over their heads.

"Thank you all for coming," George heard the king say. "I'm afraid that I have some sad news to tell you all."

George grew worried because he didn't like the thought of sad news.

"A little human girl is stuck in the cave in the woods," the Giant King continued worriedly. "She wandered into our lands and now she cannot get out."

"But how can we help her?" one of the giants in the crowd asked. "We are all too big to fit into the caves!"

Worried murmurs rippled through the crowd. The giants were a very friendly race of people and they really wanted to help the little girl but they knew that they couldn't because they were all too big to crawl into the small caves.

Gerry glanced over at his little brother. "George!" he whispered. "You might be able to fit into the caves."

"Yes, because I'm very small," George said bitterly.

"But being small is a *good* thing if you can help a little girl," Gerry said. "Why don't you try? Then, you can prove that being small can be good."

George thought about what Gerry had said. He really wanted to help the little human girl and he knew that he was the only one that would be able to fit into the caves. However, he was so scared that everyone would laugh at him for being small.

Thinking about things, George decided that he had to be brave. Even if people laughed at him for being small, he wanted to help the girl and that was more important. He would be selfless and do what he could.

George stepped forward and walked toward the stage where the king was standing. "Maybe I can help," George said.

The king stared down at him and smiled. "Yes!" he exclaimed. "You're the smallest giant I've ever seen. You'll be able to fit into the caves and rescue the human girl."

"I will go now and find her," George promised.

"If you can rescue her, you will be a hero," the king told him.

"I *will* rescue her," George said, though he didn't feel as confident as he wanted to appear.

George heard the other giants wishing him lots of luck as he started on his journey towards the woods. It wasn't a long walk but George only had little legs so it took him longer than it would take the other giants.

Finally, he reached the woods and he headed towards the caves. The entrance to the caves was so small that even George had to stoop to enter them. He crawled through the opening and shuffled through the darkness.

"Hello?" he called out, looking around as he tried to see the little girl. "Is anyone here?"

Suddenly, he heard crying and whimpering. Heading toward the noise, he saw a little girl with dark brown curls framing her tear-stained face. The girl was standing on her own holding a teddy bear in one hand. She looked at him, clearly frightened.

"Who are you?" she whispered.

"I'm George," he replied. "What's your name?"

"Sophia," she told him. "I want my mummy and daddy."

"I'll help you get back to them," he promised her. "How did you get here?"

Sophia shrugged. "I don't know," she said. "I was playing in the woods and suddenly I was in this strange land. I got scared to I came into the caves to find shelter. Where am I?"

"You're in the land of the giants," he said softly. "Our world is right next to your world. Sometimes, people from your world accidentally cross into ours."

The child looked very scared. "Giants?" she asked.

"Oh, don't worry, we're very friendly," he assured her.

Frowning she looked at him. "You don't look like a giant."

George blushed. "I'm the littlest giant. All the other giants are taller than I am."

Sophia shrugged and smiled. "Being small isn't a bad thing," she said. "I'm small and everyone loves me."

George bellowed with laughter at her words. "Why don't we get you out of here so you can go back to your family?"

He held out his hand to Sophia and she took it. The child followed him as he led her out of the caves and back into the woods. They walked in silence past all the huge oak trees that stood tall around them until they reached the border between the land of giants and the human world.

"Thank you for rescuing me," she said. "I'll never forget you."

George felt happy tears on his cheeks as he watched her cross over into her own world again. He took a deep breath and returned to the town square where everyone was waiting for him.

"I returned the human girl to her world," he announced to the King.

The crowd roared with cheers and they all admired what George had done. As he looked around at all the smiling faces, he realised that if he hadn't been small, he wouldn't have been able to save Sophia and return her to the people that loved her. Maybe being small wasn't so bad after all.

WHEN THE WITCH LEARNED A LESSON

The mean witch had ruled over the faery kingdom for many years. All the faeries disliked the mean witch because she was not very nice. She wouldn't let the faeries have fun and they just wanted to enjoy themselves.

The witch lived in a large castle at the top of a hill on the edge of the Mystic Woods but none of the faeries ever went close to the castle. They were too scared of the witch and they feared that she would stop them from being able to fly. There were many stories of the witch banishing faeries from the kingdom or taking away their wings.

The witch's power came from her wand. It was a long silver stick that she always carried with her wherever she went and she never let it out of her sight.

Amelie and Derrick were two faeries who lived in the kingdom. They were faerie twins but they were opposites in every way. Amelie was brave and loud but Derrick was shy and quiet. The one thing they both shared was a fear of the witch.

The twins were flying out by the Mystic River one morning, collecting honey for their breakfast. It was their favourite food in the whole world. They heard some horses' hooves approaching and they stopped what they were doing to see where the noise was coming from.

As they looked up, they saw four large black horses pulling an iron carriage behind them. Instantly, they recognised it as the witch's carriage and they became very scared. They decided to hide behind a tree so that the witch did not see them.

Watching the carriage pass by, they heard a loud crack as one of the wheels hit a rock. The carriage tumbled to the side and almost fell into the water. Her wand flew out of the window, rolling across the grass and landing in front of the space where Amelie and Derrick were hiding.

Staring in horror, they saw the witch jump out of the carriage in a panic. "My wand!" she screamed. "I have dropped my wand out of the carriage window when it fell onto its side. Without my wand, I am nothing!"

Before the witch could say another word, the four horses bolted and ran away into the depths of the forest leaving the witch alone by the side of the river. The witch was nothing like the twin faeries had expected her to look. They had never seen her get out of her carriage before. They thought she would be green-skinned and ugly with lots of warts but she had long chestnut hair and a complexion like the snow.

The witch sat down on a log and Amelie and Derrick decided to make sure that she was alright. Although they were scared, the witch didn't look as scary as they had thought and she had lost her wand so she couldn't hurt them. Both of the twins felt sorry for her because she looked so sad and lost.

The twins fluttered their wings and flew over to the witch. She didn't see them at first but when she saw them, she scowled.

"Faeries!" she exclaimed coldly. "What do you want?"

"We saw the carriage crash," they told her. "We wanted to make sure you're alright."

"I don't need the help of faeries," the witch said. "Go away. If I had my wand, I would banish you from this kingdom forever."

Feeling bold, Amelie flew closer to the witch. "Why do you hate faeries so much?" she asked curiously. "We never did anything bad to you."

The witch cackled menacingly. "You wouldn't understand," she said sadly.

"Why don't you explain it to us?" Amelie suggested. "My mum and dad always say that it's good to talk about your feelings when you're sad."

Sighing, the witch wrung her hands together. "When I was a little witch, I was the only witch in the whole faerie. None of the faeries wanted to be my friend because I was different from them. I always said that someday I would grow up and get my revenge."

Suddenly the twins understood why the witch was so mean to faeries. She was angry that some faeries had been mean to her when she was a little witch so she had grown up to think that all faeries were bad. Even though they knew that wasn't an excuse for being mean to people, they knew that she was just hurt about the way she had been treated.

Derrick approached the witch shyly. "I'm sorry that some faeries were mean to you," he said. "When I was a really little faery, there was another faery in my class at faery school who was mean to me. He used to pick on me because I was very shy and quiet. It made me sad and I didn't like him."

The witch looked at him curiously, her face softening. "Did you get your revenge on him?" she asked.

Derrick shook his head. "No," he replied. "I wanted to but my sister, Amelie told me that it is always better to be the bigger faery and show the mean faeries that they don't hurt you. It's always better to be kind than mean."

Amelie nodded at his side. "There are lots of mean faeries," she agreed. "But there are also lots of nice faeries. You can't judge *all* faeries because of a few mean ones. We're not mean to you, are we? We want to help you."

The witch looked very confused like she had never thought about it before. She was lost in thought for several seconds. "You're right," she said sadly. "I have spent so many years being angry about the mean faeries that I became mean too. I don't want to be mean anymore. It's very lonely because nobody likes me. I thought it would be good if everyone was scared of me but I wish I had some friends."

Amelie and Derrick grinned. "We'll be your friends," they offered at the same time, laughing and smiling.

"But, surely it's too late," the witch said. "Everyone already thinks I'm horrible and they'll always be afraid of me."

"That's not true," Amelie said. "People can change if they want to and others can change their opinions. When they see how nice you really are, they won't be scared of you anymore and they'll want to be your friends."

The witch nodded. "I'm glad I met you," she said. "I thought that crashing here in the woods and losing my wand was a very bad thing but it made me see that there are nice and kind faeries. I wish I had opened my mind earlier and not been so mean for all those years."

"That's in the past now," Derrick said. "You have changed."

"What about my wand, though?" the witch said with a sigh. "Without it, I can't undo all the mean things I've done or bring back all the faeries I banished from the kingdom."

Amelie grinned and whooshed over to the place where she'd seen the wand land. She held it out to the witch. "Do you promise that you will only use it for good now?"

Nodding, the witch took the wand. "I promise," she said before disappearing in a puff of smoke.

Over the next few weeks, the twins were very happy to hear that the witch really had changed. Everyone in the kingdom was surprised at how nice she had become. She used her magic for good instead of bad. The witch had learned her lesson and everyone came to love her for her kindness.

THE SAND IMPS

The sand imps lived in the dunes by the sea. They had a very happy life but everyone was upset by one of the imps who was always boasting about how good he was at everything

"I can run through the dunes faster than anyone else!" Irvin the imp always said. "Nobody can ever beat me."

Isaac the imp shook his head. "It's not good to be boastful, Irvin," he told him.

"Nobody wants to be around a boaster," Imogen the imp agreed.

But still, Irvin never stopped boasting. He could run faster and jump higher than everyone else, even though he would never prove it. After a while, none of the other imps wanted to be friends with Irvin because all he would do was boast about what he could do and it annoyed them.

The imps were all out having fun by the seashore when they saw Irvin racing over the dunes. They felt annoyed to see him because they were sure that he would boast about something today.

"Hello, imps," he said. "I am very proud to tell you that my mummy and daddy and I are moving to the biggest dune on the beach. It is so bigger and much bigger than any of your dunes."

Imogen crinkled her nose. "It doesn't matter how big your dune is, Irvin," she said. "What matters is that you are nice to people."

"Of course, it matters," Irvin replied. "Being the best is the only thing that counts in life."

As time went by, the imps spent less and less time around Irvin. They were tired of hearing him boast all the time. As the summer approached, news reached the imps that there was going to be a competition across the land to find the imp who could run the fastest and jump the highest.

All the imps thought that Irvin would enter the competition because he always said that he was the very best imp. So, they were surprised when they heard that he didn't want to enter.

"Why don't you enter, Irvin?" Imogen asked. "You can show everyone how you can run fast and jump high."

Ian shook his head. "I would win too easily," he said.

"So, you should prove it to everyone," suggested Isaac. "Unless you're scared."

Ian looked very unsure but he didn't want people to think that he was a cowardly imp. Truthfully, he knew that he wasn't the best runner or jumper but he couldn't think of any way out now. He'd spent so much time boasting about all the things he could do because he thought it would make people like him.

Now, he knew that they wouldn't like him at all and he would look silly when they saw that he wasn't the best imp. But, no matter how hard Irvin thought, he couldn't find an excuse not to enter the competition.

When the day of the competition finally arrived, imps from all over the land gathered around the sand dunes. The competition was the biggest that the imps had ever seen and everyone was very excited. There were lots of events and Irvin had entered the running and jumping competition. He would have to run across the sand and jump over the dunes. The imp that finished most quickly would be declared the winner.

As all the imps lined up at the start line, Irvin felt very nervous. He could see that all the other imps from his beach were watching him. He'd told them over and over again how good he was and now, he had to prove it. But he also knew that he *couldn't*. There were nine other imps in his race and they all looked like they wanted to win too.

The starter stood in front of them. "One...two...three...go!" he said.

All the imps set off running and Irvin quickly fell behind the rest. He was very tired by the time he reached the first dune. Using all his strength, he managed to jump over it but he couldn't jump very high at all. He started running again toward the second sand dune. When he reached the second dune, the other imps in the race were out of sight.

Ian started to feel worried. He knew that everyone was going to laugh at him and nobody would want to be his friend anymore because he wasn't the best runner or the highest jumper. He wanted to give up but he also realised that he had to finish the race. Struggling, Irvin ran the rest of the way and finished a long way behind all the other imps. He was glad it was over but he didn't want to face the imps.

Imogen was waiting at the finishing line and she walked over to him. "I'm sorry that you didn't win, Irvin," she said.

"I suppose you don't want to be my friend anymore because I didn't win," Irvin said sadly.

"What do you mean?" Imogen asked as Isaac came over to them too.

Ian hung his head. "Imps only want to be friends with other imps who are the best. Now that you know I'm not the best, you won't like me anymore."

Isaac laughed loudly, startling Irvin. "You're very silly, Irvin," he said. "We didn't want to be friends with you before because you were always boasting about how good you are at everything. We thought it was boring. But now that you've shown you're *not* the best, maybe you won't boast anymore."

"If you're not boasting all the time, that means we can be your friend," added Imogen with a kind smile.

Irvin was very confused and wrinkled his forehead. "So, that means you want to be my friend because I'm not as good as the other imps at running and jumping?"

"We want to be your friend if you don't boast anymore," Imogen explained. "Boasters are boring, Irvin. It's not how good you are at stuff that counts; it's the kind of imp you are that matters."

It took several moments before Irvin finally understood what they were saying. They didn't care about what he could *do*. They cared about who he was. Now, everything was clear. All those times that they hadn't wanted to play with him, it wasn't because they thought he wasn't good enough. They were just tired of his boasting. Irvin promised himself that he wouldn't boast any more.

"I'm sorry," Irvin said. "I understand now that it's important to show that I'm a good imp instead of telling everyone what I can do."

Imogen and Isaac nodded happily. "So, do you want to come and play with us in the dunes?" Isaac asked.

Irvin nodded excitedly and ran after his new friends. He didn't need to boast anymore because he saw that life was about being a good imp and deep down inside, he was the best imp there ever was.

DISCLAIMER

This book contains opinions and ideas of the author and is meant to teach the reader informative and helpful knowledge while due care should be taken by the user in the application of the information provided. The instructions and strategies are possibly not right for every reader and there is no guarantee that they work for everyone. Using this book and implementing the information/recipes therein contained is explicitly your own responsibility and risk. This work with all its contents, does not guarantee correctness, completion, quality or correctness of the provided information. Misinformation or misprints cannot be completely eliminated.

Printed in Great Britain
by Amazon